Tummy Touch Desk

Kristin Maloney
Illustrated by Miranda Mundt

ISBN: 0615648657
ISBN-13: 978-0615648651

For Jack

and Jack Smith,
Happy Reading!
☺ Ms. Maloney

Ms. Madison is always saying,

When I am trying to finish my Lego® spacecraft during morning work, she says,

"Tummy touch desk, Jack!"

If I am digging through the sharpened-pencils trying to find the only pencil that doesn't have the eraser **chewed off**, she says,

I do like Ms. Madison though.

She always gives me **snuggles** in the morning,

winks when I raise my hand instead of blurting out,

and gives me quiet time when life gets **a little hard.**

Life gets hard when you are six years old,
and Ms. Madison understands that.
What she doesn't understand is the comfy level of
our classroom chairs,

that math isn't as fun   as she thinks it is,

and that I may or may not have

ants in my pants.

If you have never been in Ms. Madison's classroom you are totally missing out.

It's like a builder's workshop, an artist's studio and a children's bookstore

all in one!

Who has time to sit tummy-touch-desk when there's so much to explore?

Let's start with Builder's Workshop;
way more fun than Writer's Workshop.

Ms. Madison has the largest collection of Legos® I have ever seen-
except at Legoland.®

There are also blocks, pokey shapes and pyramid squares.

I'm practically sitting on a construction site and Ms. Madison
expects me to sit tummy-touch-desk sorting geometric shapes?

No thank you.

Sometimes I store spacecrafts I'm working on inside my desk
so that I can finish up during
SQUIRT-
Super Quiet Uninterrupted Reading Time.

Sometimes I hide my unfinished work
in other students' desks.

Either way,

the desk fairy

always discovers my hiding spots and
my creations are back in the Lego® tub
the next day.

I think Ms. Madison
secretly puts them away,
because the desk fairy
doesn't visit

messy desks
like mine.

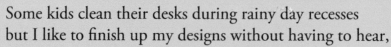

Some kids clean their desks during rainy day recesses but I like to finish up my designs without having to hear,

"Tummy touch desk, Jack!"

Jared usually acts as my assistant, helping me design my next big skyscraper.

This is a big help because usually I am on my own during class time when it's best to build.

WASHINGTON

During class time all the pieces are available.

I don't think Ms. Madison understands
that very important fact.

**It is the best time to build,
when I don't have to share the pieces.**

LEGOS®

"Tummy touch desk, Jack. It is SQUIRT time!"

LEGOS®

Operation Space Destroyer will have to wait.

Ms. Madison has a large red shelf in the back of the room filled with the fanciest paper I have ever seen.

Usually, while everyone has their nose in a book, I pretend as if I'm going to the water cooler, but I quietly grab some paper-

reds, blues and some greens.

I quickly hurry back, sit tummy-touch-desk

-check that out-
and grab a pair of scissors.

The fancy paper is perfect for cutting
because it is not too flimsy but still quite easy to fold.

I cut out several different shapes.
After I have a few shapes, I take
a black marker and write a
large X inside each shape.

This is my secret symbol.

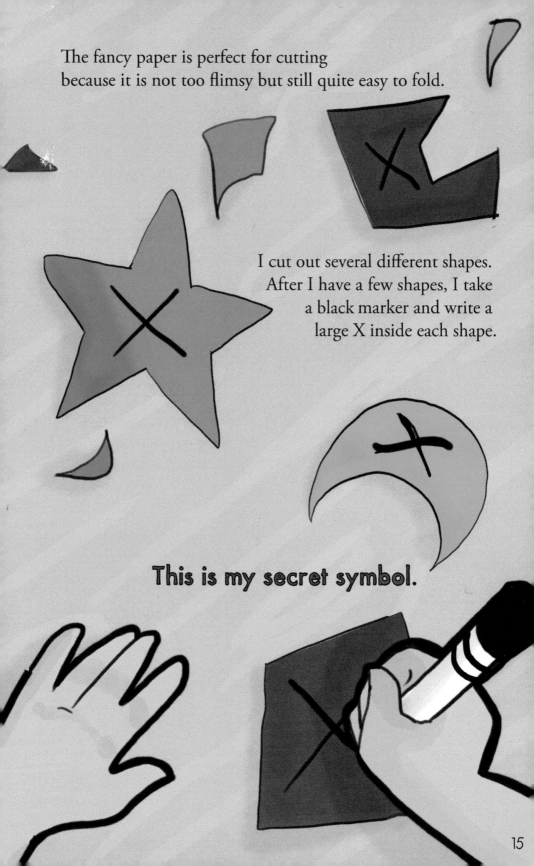

The next part is tricky; getting the tape,

like a secret agent, without being seen.

Ms. Madison says I am a tape waster. She doesn't understand that you can never use too much tape. Tape makes or breaks any kind of art project! She always says,

"Jack, are you taping the whole world, or just a piece of paper?"

Hmmm... the whole world...
that would be an amazing project!

I slowly get up out of my chair, the lights are low
so I am sure no one can see me,
and wander over to the supply table.

Ms. Madison is reading with Joe
so she won't see me at all.

I string out a **looooong** strip of tape and hear,

19

I slowly walk back to my desk, tape behind my back, careful not to twist it-

SCISSORS

Earliest scissors date to Mesopotamia 3,000 to 4,000 years ago

if it twists and sticks to itself,
it is useless to me.

I slump back into my uncomfy chair
and start snipping the long strands of tape in to
smaller, inchworm sized pieces.

DID YOU KNOW?
Inchworms are
larva of

Geometer Moths

This is the best part. While the rest of the class is distracted by their books, I slink around the room like a snake, careful not to get noticed.

I begin sticking a magic shape with my secret symbol onto the other kids' desks. By the time they discover the magic work of art,

I will be long gone and never be suspected.

I have become so good at slithering around the classroom, I am practically invisible. Only two more desks to go.

I hear a raspy high whisper above me.
Busted. I am discovered.

Jake looks down at me as I lay on my elbows on the floor.

"Stop crawling around. Ms. Madison will be so grumpy if she finds you!"

Jake always discovers my missions.
I don't think my Super Invisible Powers work on him.

I slip back to my desk, even managing to stick a shape
on Ms. Madison's desk on the way.
Success. I didn't get caught.

Jake doesn't really count
'cause he's not the boss of me.

Recess bell rings.

I grab my snack and bolt out the door. As I leave,
I notice my magic shapes are being discovered.
No one will ever suspect it was me.

Last recess is always the most fun recess because first graders get the play structures all to themselves.

I'm always a little sleepy after a recess of wizards and dragons. It's really hard work.

You're out if you touch the wood chips!

Once in from recess,
we have to work in our reading workbooks.

This is the perfect time to make my books.

I carefully take, I mean, borrow Ms. Madison's stapler, grab some colored paper and...

Ah! How on earth does this lady always know where I am!?

I mope back to my desk, stapler in my pocket, paper behind my back.
Time to write my story. I know I should be doing my workbook but I like writing my own stories a lot better than reading other people's stories.

Sound out your Words!

BALL-oon
Balloon
1. Look for small words in big words.
2. STRETCH out the word.
B All-Ll-oo-n

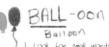

I brainstorm - that's a teacher word.

I carefully staple my pages together to make a book;
watching to make sure my fingers are clear-

last time that really hurt!

Voilà! I have created my book! Now I just have to write a story.

Okay, main character; **boy**.

Problem;
Too much to do, too little time.
Uncomfortable chair.

Solution;
first grade boy
saves planet.

Hmm...
that doesn't sound right.

I need an eraser.
Spotted. Pink eraser under Jamie's desk. I slither over.
I feel Jake kick my left leg,

"Tummy touch desk, Jack!"

What!
Does he think he is the ruler of the world?

While slithering back to my desk, I rest my head on the reading rug.

My eyes are feeling sleepy. It gets quiet...

I hear Ms. Madison talking about synonyms and...
it sounds like cinnamon.

Yum.

I love cinnamon; I should name my new story Cinnamon.

Cinnamon Boy saves planet.
Nope. Not good.

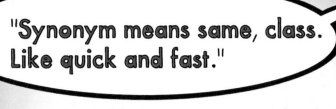

"Synonym means same, class. Like quick and fast."

A boy with superpowers saves the classroom
with his quick slithering.
Hmmm...My eyes begin to close...

save us snake boy!!!

Stay awaaaaake!
Must think of a good name for my next book...
What would best describe me... I need a title...I drift off.

I hear Ms. Madison loud and clear, she wakes me out of my snooze.

THE END

16846707R10025

Made in the USA
Charleston, SC
13 January 2013